Inspirational stories for amazing kids

NASHWAN HASAN

Published by NASHWAN HASAN, 2023.

This is a work of fiction. Similarities to real people, places, or events are entirely coincidental.

INSPIRATIONAL STORIES FOR AMAZING KIDS

First edition. March 29, 2023.

Written by NASHWAN HASAN.

Inspirational stories

Welcome to a world of wonder, where you can join in on thrilling adventures and learn valuable lessons along the way.

This book is a collection of inspiring stories that will captivate young readers and ignite their imagination. These tales are filled with fascinating characters who demonstrate courage, kindness, and perseverance in the face of adversity.

Whether you are a young reader just beginning your journey into the world of literature, or an experienced reader seeking a new source of inspiration, these stories will uplift your spirit and nourish your soul. From stories about magical creatures and brave heroes to tales of ordinary people who overcome great challenges, this book has something for everyone.

Each story is unique, but they all share a common theme: the power of the human spirit to triumph over adversity.

These stories will encourage children to dream big, believe in themselves, and never give up. So come along on a journey of discovery and inspiration, and be prepared to be amazed by the incredible tales that await you in this book.

Abandoned house

Once upon a time, in a magical land far, far away, there lived a little girl named Lily. Lily was a curious and adventurous child who loved exploring the world around her. She would often wander off into the woods, climb trees, and chase butterflies.

One day, while wandering through the forest, Lily stumbled upon an old, abandoned house.

The house was rundown and covered in vines, but there was something about it that intrigued Lily. She decided to investigate.

As she approached the house, she noticed that there was a sign hanging on the front door. The sign read: "Welcome to the House of Dreams. Enter if you dare."

Lily hesitated for a moment, but her curiosity got the best of her, and she pushed the door open. As she stepped inside, she was surrounded by darkness. But as her eyes adjusted to the dim light, she saw that the walls were covered in colorful murals and the floor was made of soft, plush grass.

Suddenly, she heard a voice calling out to her. "Welcome, Lily," the voice said. "I am the Keeper of Dreams. I have been waiting for you."

Lily was amazed. She had never heard of the Keeper of Dreams before, but she was eager to learn more.

The Keeper of Dreams explained to Lily that she was the chosen one. She had been chosen to enter the House of Dreams because of her curious and adventurous spirit. The Keeper of Dreams told Lily that she had the power to make her dreams come true.

Lily was thrilled. She had always had big dreams, but she never knew how to make them a reality. The Keeper of Dreams showed Lily how to use her imagination to create the world she wanted to live in.

From that day on, Lily visited the House of Dreams every day. She would explore the rooms, play with the magical creatures, and learn from the Keeper of Dreams. And with every visit, her dreams became more and more real.

Years passed, and Lily grew up to be a brave and imaginative woman. She used the lessons she learned in the House of Dreams to create a life she loved. And she always remembered to thank the Keeper of Dreams for showing her the way.

So remember, children, never stop dreaming. And always remember that with a little bit of imagination, anything is possible. Who knows? Maybe you'll even stumble upon the House of Dreams one day.

Great explorer

Once upon a time, in a faraway land, there was a young boy named Jack who dreamed of becoming a great explorer. He spent hours poring over maps and reading books about far-off lands, dreaming of the adventures he would one day have.

But Jack's family was poor, and they lived in a small village where no one ever left. His parents urged him to forget about his dreams and focus on more practical matters, like helping with the family's farm. But Jack refused to give up on his dreams. He knew that one day, he would find a way to explore the world.

One day, Jack heard about a famous explorer who was passing through the nearby city. He begged his parents for permission to go meet him, and after much pleading, they finally relented. Jack set out on foot, determined to meet the explorer and learn all he could from him.

When Jack arrived at the city, he found the explorer's tent and approached him timidly. The explorer was kind and gracious, and he listened patiently as Jack told him about his dreams of exploring the world. To Jack's surprise, the explorer offered to take him on his next expedition.

Jack was overjoyed, but his parents were hesitant. They worried about their son leaving on a dangerous adventure with a stranger. But Jack begged them to let him go, promising to return safely and with great stories to tell.

And so, Jack set out on the adventure of a lifetime. He sailed across the ocean, hiked through dense jungles, and climbed towering mountains. He saw things he never imagined and met people from all corners of the world. Along the way, he learned important lessons about courage, kindness, and determination.

When Jack returned home, he was a changed person. He was more confident, more curious, and more determined than ever before.

He knew that there was a big world out there waiting to be explored, and he was ready to see it all.

And so, Jack became a famous explorer in his own right. He traveled the world, charting new territories and discovering new wonders. And he never forgot the lessons he learned on his first great adventure – the power of dreams, the importance of perseverance, and the beauty of the world around us.

Small village

Once upon a time, in a faraway land, there was a small village nestled in the foothills of a majestic mountain range. The village was a happy place, with its friendly people, colorful houses, and bustling marketplace. In this village, there was a little girl named Maya. Maya was a curious and adventurous girl who loved exploring the world around her. She was always eager to learn new things and make new friends. One day, as she was playing by the river, Maya noticed something unusual. There was a small fish struggling to swim against the current. Maya felt sorry for the fish and knew that it needed her help.

Without hesitation, she jumped into the river and swam towards the fish. She scooped it up in her hands and gently placed it on the shore. The fish was weak and tired, but with Maya's help, it started to recover. As she watched the fish swim away,

Maya realized something important. Even the smallest act of kindness can make a big difference in someone's life. From that day on, Maya made it her mission to help anyone in need. She spent her days volunteering at the local hospital, helping her neighbors with their chores, and even teaching younger children how to read and write. Over time, Maya's acts of kindness inspired others to do the same. The village became a more caring and compassionate place, where everyone looked out for each other and worked together to make the world a better place. And so, Maya learned that even though she was just a little girl, she had the power to make a difference in the world. She knew that by helping others, she could make the world a brighter and happier place for everyone.

Adventurous child

Once upon a time, in a faraway land, there was a young boy named Max. Max was an adventurous and curious child, always eager to explore and learn new things. One day, while exploring the forest near his home, Max stumbled upon a small bird with a broken wing.

Feeling sorry for the bird, Max took it back to his house and cared for it until its wing was healed. As a thank you, the bird offered to take Max on a magical adventure.

The bird revealed that it was no ordinary bird, but a magical creature known as a phoenix. The phoenix explained to Max that it possessed the ability to grant him a single wish.

Overwhelmed by the offer, Max spent many days thinking about what he would wish for. He could ask for anything in the world, but he wanted to make sure that his wish would make a difference.

Finally, Max decided on his wish. He asked the phoenix to grant him the power to help others. He didn't want to be rich or famous, but he wanted to make a difference in the world.

The phoenix was pleased with Max's selfless wish and granted him the power to help others. From that day on, Max dedicated his life to helping those in need. He volunteered at the local hospital, helped out at the animal shelter, and even started a charity to help children in impoverished countries.

Max's selflessness and dedication to helping others inspired people all around the world. He became known as a hero and was loved by everyone who knew him.

Years went by, and Max grew old, but he never stopped helping others. As he lay on his deathbed, surrounded by loved ones, the phoenix appeared once again.

The phoenix congratulated Max on a life well-lived and thanked him for using his wish to help others. In that moment, Max realized that the true magic was not in the wish itself, but in the power of kindness and compassion.

And so, Max passed away with a smile on his face, knowing that he had made a difference in the world. The phoenix took flight and soared into the sky, leaving behind a trail of sparkling feathers as a reminder of Max's inspiring legacy.

Magical forest

Once upon a time, in a magical forest, there lived a small rabbit named Rosie. Rosie was very kind and loved to help her friends in the forest. She would spend her days gathering food and helping the other animals with their tasks.

One day, Rosie heard about a big race that was going to take place in the forest. All of the animals were excited to participate, and Rosie wanted to join in too. However, she was worried that she wouldn't be fast enough to keep up with the other animals.

Rosie's best friend, a wise old owl named Oliver, noticed her worries and decided to help.

Oliver reminded Rosie that she didn't have to be the fastest to win the race, and that her kindness and helpfulness would be more valuable than speed.

With Oliver's encouragement, Rosie decided to join the race. The day of the race arrived, and all the animals gathered at the starting line. Rosie felt nervous as she looked at the other animals, who were all much bigger and faster than her.

But as the race began, something amazing happened. The other animals began to encounter obstacles on the course, and Rosie was there to help them. She helped a squirrel who had gotten his tail stuck in a tree, and she showed a lost bird the way back to her nest.

As Rosie reached the finish line, all of the animals cheered for her. They realized that Rosie's kindness and helpfulness had made her the true winner of the race.

From that day on, Rosie continued to help her friends in the forest, and they all looked up to her as a role model. Rosie learned that being kind and helpful was more important than being fast or strong, and that true success comes from helping others.

And so, Rosie the rabbit lived happily ever after, inspiring generations of animals to be kind and helpful to one another.

Mia in the jungle

Once upon a time, in a far-off land, there lived a little girl named Mia. Mia was a curious child who loved exploring and learning about the world around her. She spent most of her days playing in the fields, climbing trees, and chasing butterflies.

One day, while playing in the woods, Mia came across a small bird lying on the ground. The bird had a broken wing and was unable to fly. Mia knew she had to help the bird, so she gently picked it up and brought it home.

Mia cared for the bird, feeding it and making sure it was comfortable. Over time, the bird's wing healed, and it was able to fly again. The bird was so grateful to Mia for her kindness that it decided to stay with her and be her companion.

Mia was overjoyed to have a new friend, and together, they went on many adventures. They explored the woods, climbed mountains, and swam in the rivers. The bird was always by Mia's side, encouraging her to try new things and be brave.

One day, while they were exploring a nearby cave, Mia and her bird friend came across a group of lost travelers. The travelers had been wandering in the cave for days and were unable to find their way out. Mia knew she had to help them, so she used her knowledge of the cave and her bravery to guide them out safely.

The travelers were so grateful to Mia that they threw her a big celebration and declared her a hero. Mia was proud of herself and her accomplishments, but she knew that it was her kindness and her willingness to help that made her a hero.

From that day on, Mia continued to explore the world with her bird friend, but she also made it her mission to help others and be a force for good in the world. She knew that even a small act of kindness could make a big difference and that everyone has the power to be a hero.

Little bird and owl

Once upon a time, in a small village nestled in the heart of a forest, there lived a little bird named Tweetie. Tweetie was a curious and adventurous bird who loved to explore the forest and meet new friends.

One day, Tweetie set out on an adventure to explore a nearby mountain. As she flew higher and higher, she felt her wings growing tired, but she refused to give up. Finally, she reached the top of the mountain and was amazed by the breathtaking view. However, as she looked down, she realized that she had flown so high that she couldn't remember the way back to her village.

Feeling scared and alone, Tweetie began to cry. But just then, a wise old owl appeared and asked her what was wrong. Tweetie explained her predicament, and the owl replied, "Don't worry, little one. You may have lost your way, but you haven't lost your spirit of adventure."

The owl then told Tweetie a secret. He said, "The best way to find your way home is to follow your heart. You see, your heart will always lead you in the right direction, no matter how lost you may feel."

Feeling inspired, Tweetie wiped away her tears and decided to trust her heart. She closed her eyes and listened carefully. Soon enough, she heard a faint sound that she recognized as the song of her best friend, a blue jay named Blue. Tweetie followed the sound and was overjoyed to find Blue waiting for her at the edge of the forest.

From that day forward, Tweetie never forgot the lesson she had learned. She continued to explore the forest and make new friends, always following her heart and trusting in her spirit of adventure.

And so, dear children, the moral of the story is this: no matter where life takes you, always trust in your heart and never give up on your dreams. Just like Tweetie, you too can achieve great things if you believe in yourself and keep your spirit of adventure alive.

The little seed

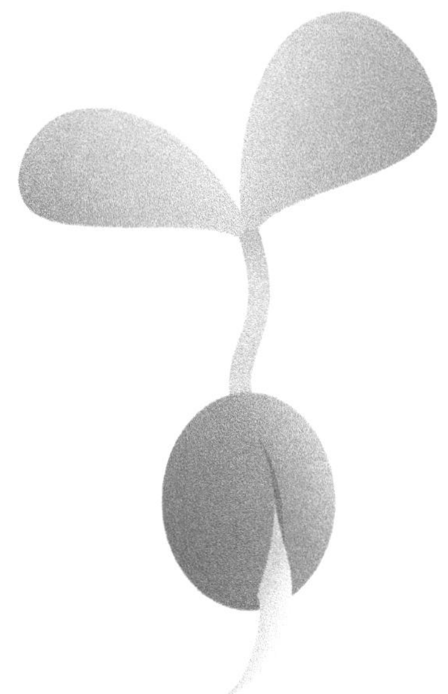

Once upon a time, there was a little seed that was nestled in the soft soil, waiting for the perfect moment to grow. As time went by, the little seed watched as other plants around it grew tall and strong, but it remained small and insignificant.

One day, a little girl came walking by and noticed the little seed. She gently picked it up and took it home with her, placing it in a small pot filled with soil. The little seed was afraid and uncertain of what was to come, but the girl whispered encouraging words to it every day, telling it that it could grow to be anything it wanted to be.

Days turned into weeks, and the little seed began to sprout, pushing its way through the soil and reaching towards the light. It grew and grew, becoming stronger with each passing day.

The girl watched with amazement as the little seed turned into a beautiful plant, with leaves that shone in the sun and flowers that bloomed in vibrant colors.

The plant was so happy and proud of itself for what it had become, but it never forgot the little girl who had believed in it when it was just a tiny seed. It always remembered the encouraging words she had whispered, and it knew that it was because of her belief in it that it had grown into something beautiful.

From that day on, the plant spread its seeds far and wide, hoping to inspire other little seeds to believe in themselves and to never give up, even when things seem difficult. It wanted to spread the message that with a little bit of patience, love, and encouragement, anything is possible.

And so, the little seed grew into a beautiful plant, not just for itself, but for all the other little seeds out there that needed a little bit of inspiration to grow into something great.

Little bird Pip

Once upon a time, in a faraway land, there was a little bird named Pip. Pip was a tiny bird, but he had big dreams. He wanted to explore the world and see all the beautiful things that he had heard about in stories.

Pip's family lived in a big tree, where all the birds in the forest made their homes. Every day, Pip would watch as the other birds flew off into the distance, exploring new places and discovering new things. Pip longed to join them, but he was too scared.

One day, as Pip was sitting on a branch, he saw a butterfly fluttering by. The butterfly was so colorful and graceful that Pip couldn't help but watch in awe. Suddenly, the butterfly turned to Pip and said, "Why do you sit here all day when you could be flying high like us?

Don't be afraid, little bird. Believe in yourself and spread your wings!"

Pip was startled but also inspired by the butterfly's words. He decided that he wouldn't let fear hold him back any longer.

He spread his wings and took off into the sky, flying higher and higher than he ever thought possible.

As he soared above the trees, Pip saw things he had never seen before. He saw sparkling rivers and towering mountains, and he felt the wind rushing through his feathers. Pip realized that there was a whole world out there waiting to be discovered, and he was determined to see it all.

From that day on, Pip never looked back. He flew over mountains, valleys, and oceans, and he met creatures of all shapes and sizes. He made new friends, and he learned many valuable lessons along the way.

Pip's courage and determination taught him that anything was possible if he just believed in himself.

He inspired other birds to follow their dreams too, and together they explored the world with wide eyes and open hearts.

And so, Pip the little bird, who once thought he was too small and afraid to fly, proved that anyone can achieve their dreams if they just have the courage to spread their wings and take flight.

Old box

Once upon a time, in a far-off land, there was a small village nestled at the foot of a great mountain. In this village lived a young boy named Tom. Tom was a curious child who loved to explore and discover new things. He would often spend his days wandering through the nearby forests, climbing trees, and watching birds.

One day, while wandering through the forest, Tom stumbled upon an old, dilapidated building. The building was so old that it looked as if it would fall apart at any moment. Curiosity getting the best of him, Tom decided to investigate the building.

As he walked inside, he was greeted by a strange sight. The walls of the building were covered in strange symbols and markings. In the center of the room was an old chest.

Tom approached the chest and found that it was locked tight. Determined to discover what was inside, he set to work on opening the lock.

After many attempts, Tom finally managed to open the chest. To his amazement, inside he found an ancient book. The book was filled with stories of brave knights, fearless adventurers, and magical creatures.

Tom was fascinated by the stories in the book. He read and reread them, imagining himself as the hero of each adventure. As he read, he began to dream of his own adventures and the exciting things he could discover.

Tom decided that he wanted to explore the mountain that overlooked his village. He had heard stories of a great dragon that lived atop the mountain and guarded a treasure trove of gold and jewels. Tom knew that this was his chance to become a real adventurer.

Gathering his courage, Tom set out on his journey up the mountain. The climb was difficult and treacherous, but Tom was determined to reach the top. When he finally reached the summit, he saw the dragon for the first time. It was a fierce creature, with scales as hard as steel and eyes that glowed like fire.

But Tom did not falter. He remembered the stories in his book and the brave knights who faced their fears. Drawing upon his courage and determination, Tom confronted the dragon.

To his surprise, the dragon did not attack. Instead, it spoke to him in a gentle voice. "Why have you come to my lair, young adventurer?" it asked.

Tom told the dragon of his love for adventure and his desire to explore the world. The dragon listened intently and then offered Tom a challenge. "If you can answer my riddle, I will give you a treasure beyond your wildest dreams," the dragon said.

Tom thought carefully and then answered the riddle. The dragon was impressed by his quick thinking and bravery. "You have proven yourself a worthy adventurer," it said. "Take this treasure and go forth to discover new and exciting things."

With that, the dragon gave Tom a small chest filled with gold and jewels. Tom was overjoyed. He thanked the dragon and set out on his journey back down the mountain.

As he made his way back to the village, Tom realized that the greatest treasure he had gained was not the gold and jewels, but the knowledge that he had the courage and determination to face his fears and explore the world.

And so, Tom continued to explore and discover new things. He became known throughout the land as a brave and fearless adventurer, and his stories inspired many other children to follow in his footsteps.

King of the jungle

Once upon a time, in the heart of the African savannah, there was a majestic lion named Leo. He was known as the king of the jungle, as he was strong, brave, and wise. Leo had a beautiful mane of golden fur, sharp teeth, and a powerful roar that could be heard for miles around.

Leo lived with his family in a vast territory, where they roamed free and hunted together. He was a respected leader among his pride, and all the animals of the savannah looked up to him for guidance and protection.

One day, Leo heard the news that a fierce pack of hyenas was attacking the weaker animals in the nearby forest. He knew that he had to act fast to stop them, so he called for a meeting with the other animals of the savannah.

As they gathered around him, Leo spoke with a deep, commanding voice. "My friends," he said, "we cannot let the hyenas continue to prey on the weak and defenseless. We must stand together and defend our land and our fellow creatures."

The other animals listened to Leo's words and nodded in agreement. They knew that he was right and that they had to act fast to stop the hyenas from causing more harm.

Leo then led the charge into the forest, followed by a group of elephants, rhinoceroses, and other powerful animals. They roared and trumpeted, creating a cacophony of sound that echoed throughout the savannah.

The hyenas were taken aback by the sudden attack, but they did not back down. They snarled and bared their teeth, ready to fight to the death.

Leo stepped forward, his mane blowing in the wind. He looked at the hyenas with a fierce determination and let out a deafening roar. The hyenas quivered in fear, realizing that they had met their match.

In a matter of minutes, the hyenas were defeated and chased out of the forest. The other animals cheered and congratulated Leo for his bravery and leadership.

From that day on, Leo became a legend in the savannah, and his story was told for generations to come. Children would listen in awe as they heard about the lion who stood up to the hyenas and saved the weaker animals.

And every time they looked at the golden sun setting behind the trees, they would see the silhouette of a proud lion, standing tall and strong, ready to protect his land and his fellow creatures.

Little mouse

Once upon a time, in a far-off land, there lived a little mouse named Mia. Mia was a curious little mouse who loved to explore the world around her. One day, while she was out gathering food, she stumbled upon a beautiful garden. It was full of vibrant flowers, sweet-smelling herbs, and towering trees that seemed to touch the sky.

Mia had never seen such a magnificent place before, and she couldn't wait to explore it. As she began to walk through the garden, she noticed a group of other animals gathered around a tree. She scurried over to join them and saw that they were all staring up at a branch high above their heads.

"What are you all looking at?" Mia asked.

"We're watching the birds," said a wise old owl who was perched on a nearby branch. "They come here every day to sing and play in the tree."

Mia looked up and saw a group of birds perched on the branch, singing and chirping to each other. She was amazed by their beautiful songs and wished she could join in.

"I want to learn how to sing like the birds," Mia said.

The other animals looked at her skeptically. "But you're just a mouse," they said. "You can't sing like the birds."

Mia didn't let their doubts discourage her. She was determined to learn how to sing like the birds, no matter what anyone else thought. So, every day, she would climb up to the top of the tree and listen to the birds singing. She would practice for hours, trying to mimic their songs and learn their techniques.

At first, it was difficult. Mia's tiny voice couldn't match the birds' beautiful melodies. But she didn't give up. She kept practicing every day, determined to achieve her dream.

As time went on, Mia's voice grew stronger and clearer. Her notes became more accurate, and her melodies more intricate. And soon enough, she was singing just as beautifully as the birds.

The other animals in the garden were amazed. They had never heard a mouse sing like that before. They all gathered around Mia, cheering and applauding her for her hard work and determination.

From that day on, Mia continued to sing and explore the garden, sharing her beautiful voice with all the creatures she met. And she learned that if you set your mind to something and work hard, you can achieve anything you want, no matter how small or unlikely you may seem.

Dragon and David

Once upon a time, in a far-off land, there lived a brave boy named David. He was an adventurous and curious child, always seeking to explore the world around him. Despite his young age, David had already faced many challenges and had emerged victorious each time.

David's bravery was put to the test one day when a terrible dragon attacked his village. The dragon was enormous, with scales as black as night and eyes that glowed like hot coals. It breathed fire and smoke, and its roar shook the earth.

The villagers were terrified and didn't know what to do. They huddled together in fear, waiting for the dragon to attack. But David was not afraid. He knew that he had to do something to save his people.

He thought carefully about what he could do to defeat the dragon. He remembered a story his grandfather had told him about a great warrior who defeated a dragon by using its own strength against it.

With this idea in mind, David set out to find the dragon. He walked for many miles through dark forests and across rushing rivers until he finally came to the dragon's lair.

The dragon was waiting for him, its eyes blazing with anger. David stood his ground, his heart pounding with fear but his determination stronger than ever.

The dragon lunged at him, breathing fire, but David dodged out of the way. He circled around the dragon, watching its movements carefully. He waited for the right moment, and then he charged at the dragon, grabbing hold of its tail.

The dragon thrashed and roared, trying to shake David off, but he held on tight. As the dragon flung itself around, David used its momentum to pull it off-balance. With a mighty heave, he threw the dragon to the ground.

The dragon lay there, stunned, as David stood over it, ready to strike. But as he looked into the dragon's eyes, he saw something he had not expected. He saw fear and sadness, and he realized that the dragon was not evil, but only frightened and alone.

David put down his sword and approached the dragon, speaking softly to it. He touched the dragon's scales gently and felt its body relax under his touch. The dragon looked up at him, and David saw gratitude in its eyes.

With the dragon's help, David was able to lead it back to the village, where the people were amazed to see the once-terrifying creature now under the boy's control.

The villagers realized that David's bravery and compassion had saved them all, and they honored him with a great feast and many gifts. From that day forward, David was known throughout the land as the bravest boy who ever lived.

And even though he faced many challenges and battles in the years to come, he never forgot the lesson he learned that day: that true bravery comes not from strength and weapons, but from kindness and compassion.

Evil sorcerer

Once upon a time, in a faraway kingdom, there lived a young boy named Jack. Jack was a brave and adventurous boy who lived in a small village on the outskirts of the kingdom.

One day, the kingdom was threatened by a powerful and evil sorcerer who had come to conquer the land. The sorcerer had a fierce army of magical creatures at his disposal and was determined to destroy the kingdom and take over the land.

The people of the kingdom were terrified and helpless, but Jack was not. He knew that he had to do something to protect his home and his people. So, he decided to take matters into his own hands and go on a mission to defeat the evil sorcerer.

Jack set out on his journey, carrying nothing but his bravery and determination. As he traveled through the forest, he met a group of friendly animals who offered to help him on his mission. A wise owl, a fierce wolf, and a clever fox joined him on his journey, and together they set off to face the sorcerer.

As they approached the sorcerer's castle, Jack and his animal friends were faced with a terrifying army of magical creatures. But Jack did not falter. He drew his sword and charged fearlessly into battle, with the animals by his side.

The battle was fierce and intense, but Jack and his animal friends fought bravely, and slowly but surely, they began to gain the upper hand. Jack used his wits and quick thinking to outsmart the sorcerer's army, while the animals used their unique abilities to help defeat the enemy.

Finally, they reached the sorcerer himself, and a fierce battle ensued. The sorcerer was powerful and had many tricks up his sleeve, but Jack and his friends were determined to win. They fought with all their might, and in the end, Jack delivered the final blow, defeating the sorcerer once and for all.

The kingdom was saved, and the people rejoiced. Jack was hailed as a hero, and he received many honors and awards for his bravery and valor. But for Jack, the greatest reward was knowing that he had helped protect his home and his people.

From that day forward, Jack was known throughout the kingdom as the bravest boy who had ever lived. He had shown that even a young boy could make a difference in the world if he had the courage and determination to do so. And so, his story became a legend, inspiring generations of young boys and girls to follow in his footsteps and become brave heroes themselves.

The only survivor

In the heart of a vast kingdom, there lived a boy named Oliver. Oliver was unlike any other boy in the kingdom. He was brave, kind, and adventurous, always looking for ways to help others.

Oliver's bravery came from a traumatic event that occurred when he was younger. His family had been attacked by a group of robbers, and he was the only survivor. Ever since that day, Oliver had vowed to use his bravery to help others and make the kingdom a safer place.

One day, while wandering through the forest, Oliver came across a group of travelers who had been robbed by bandits. The travelers were distraught and helpless, and Oliver knew he had to act quickly.

Without hesitation, Oliver picked up his sword and headed towards the bandits' hideout. The bandits were a group of ruthless thieves who had been terrorizing the kingdom for months. But Oliver was not afraid.

He sneaked into the hideout and took out the guards one by one, using his wit and cunning to outsmart them. When he finally reached the leader of the bandits, a fierce-looking man with a scar on his face, Oliver drew his sword and prepared for a fight.

The battle was intense, but Oliver's bravery and skill with a sword proved to be too much for the bandit leader. In the end, Oliver emerged victorious, and the bandits were defeated.

The travelers were overjoyed and grateful to Oliver for saving them from the clutches of the bandits. They thanked him profusely and offered him a reward, but Oliver refused. He knew that he didn't do it for the reward, but to help those in need.

Word of Oliver's bravery spread throughout the kingdom, and people began to seek him out for help with various problems. Oliver never turned anyone away, no matter how big or small the task. He believed that everyone deserved a chance to live their life to the fullest, and he did everything in his power to make that possible.

One day, the king of the kingdom summoned Oliver to his palace. The king had heard of Oliver's bravery and wanted to offer him a position in the royal army. Oliver was honored by the king's offer but refused, saying that his place was with the people of the kingdom, helping them in any way he could.

The king was impressed by Oliver's selflessness and bravery and decided to make him a knight. Oliver was thrilled and humbled by the king's offer and accepted the title with pride.

From that day forward, Oliver became known as Sir Oliver, the bravest knight in the kingdom. He continued to help those in need, always putting the safety and well-being of others above his own.

Years went by, and Sir Oliver grew old. But even in his old age, he continued to serve the people of the kingdom, always ready to lend a helping hand. When he passed away, the people of the kingdom mourned his loss but celebrated his life and the impact he had on the kingdom.

And so, Sir Oliver's bravery and selflessness became a legend in the kingdom, inspiring generations of people to be brave and kind, just like he was.

The lion and the mouse

Once upon a time, in a lush green forest filled with all sorts of animals, there lived a mighty lion. He was the king of the forest, feared and respected by all who lived there. One day, while taking a nap under a shady tree, the lion felt a tickling sensation on his paw. He woke up with a start and found a tiny mouse nibbling on his paw.

The lion was angry and roared, "How dare you disturb my rest, you tiny creature!" The mouse was terrified and pleaded with the lion to spare his life. He promised that he would repay the lion's kindness someday.

The lion laughed at the mouse's words and let him go. He thought that such a tiny creature could never be of any help to him.

A few days later, while out on a hunt, the lion was caught in a hunter's trap. He roared and struggled, but could not break free from the trap. The other animals in the forest heard his cries and came to see what had happened.

The mouse, who had been watching from a distance, saw the lion's plight and remembered his promise. He scurried up to the lion and began to gnaw at the ropes that held him captive. It took him a while, but he managed to free the lion.

The lion was amazed and grateful. He had never thought that a tiny mouse could be of such help to him. He apologized to the mouse for underestimating him and thanked him for saving his life.

From that day forward, the lion and the mouse became the best of friends. They would often be seen playing together in the forest, much to the amazement of the other animals.

The story of the lion and the mouse spread throughout the forest and beyond. People marveled at the friendship between two creatures that were so different from each other. They realized that it was not the size or strength of a creature that mattered, but the kindness and courage within.

The lion and the mouse's story became a symbol of hope and friendship, inspiring young and old alike to be kind and compassionate to all creatures great and small.

And so, the lion and the mouse lived happily ever after, their friendship a shining example of the power of kindness and compassion in the world.

Tom

Once upon a time, in a small village nestled at the foot of a great mountain range, there lived a young boy named Tom. Tom was known throughout the village as a kind and helpful soul, but he had a secret - he had a habit of telling lies.

Tom would tell tall tales about his adventures and accomplishments, often exaggerating his stories to make them sound more exciting. His friends would listen in amazement, but deep down they knew that Tom was not telling the truth.

One day, Tom was walking through the village when he came across an old man who was struggling to carry a heavy load.

Tom offered to help, but the old man refused, saying that he did not trust Tom because he had heard that he was a liar.

Tom was ashamed and realized that his habit of lying was starting to catch up with him. He began to understand the consequences of his actions - people no longer trusted him and he was losing the respect of his friends and family.

Determined to make things right, Tom decided to turn over a new leaf. He vowed to be honest and truthful from that day forward, no matter how difficult it might be.

At first, it was hard for Tom to break the habit of lying. He found himself slipping back into old patterns, but he kept reminding himself of the importance of honesty and the consequences of his actions.

Slowly but surely, Tom began to gain the trust and respect of those around him. His friends noticed the change in him and started to take him more seriously. His parents were proud of the responsible and honest young man he was becoming.

Years went by, and Tom grew up to be a successful and respected member of the community. He knew that it was his commitment to honesty and truthfulness that had gotten him there.

Tom's story became well-known throughout the village and beyond. It became a symbol of the importance of honesty and the consequences of lying. People learned that even the smallest of lies can have big consequences, but that it is never too late to change and make things right.

And so, Tom lived a long and happy life, always true to his word and never telling a lie again. His story inspired many young and old alike to be honest and truthful, no matter what the situation might be.

Monkey and rabbit

Once upon a time, in a small village surrounded by rolling hills and lush green forests, there lived two best friends - a monkey named Milo and a rabbit named Benny. Milo and Benny were inseparable. They would spend hours playing together in the fields, climbing trees, and exploring the countryside.

One day, as they were playing by the river, they noticed a fish that had washed up on the bank. The fish was gasping for air, and Milo and Benny knew that it was in trouble.

Without hesitation, Benny jumped into the river and swam to the fish.

He carefully picked it up in his teeth and brought it back to the bank. Milo, meanwhile, gathered some leaves and made a small bed for the fish.

The fish was grateful for their help and thanked them for saving its life. From that day forward, the fish became an important part of their friendship. They would often visit the fish by the river, bringing it food and water and playing games with it.

As time went on, Milo and Benny grew older, and their friendship only grew stronger. They supported each other through thick and thin, always there to lend a helping hand or a listening ear.

One day, Milo fell ill. He was unable to move or eat, and he was in a lot of pain. Benny was beside himself with worry. He knew that his friend was in trouble, but he didn't know what to do.

Just then, the fish appeared by their side. It had grown much bigger since they first saved it, and it had become a wise and kind creature. It asked Benny what was wrong, and Benny explained about Milo's illness.

The fish thought for a moment and then said, "I know of a special herb that grows on the other side of the river. It has healing properties that can cure any illness. But I cannot swim that far. You must go and get it for your friend."

Without hesitation, Benny jumped into the river and began to swim to the other side. It was a difficult journey, and he faced many challenges along the way, but he never gave up. Finally, he found the herb and brought it back to Milo.

Thanks to Benny's determination and the fish's wisdom, Milo was soon back to his old self. He was grateful to his best friend and the fish for their help.

The story of Milo, Benny, and the fish became well-known throughout the village and beyond. It became a symbol of the power of true friendship - the kind that stands the test of time and goes beyond boundaries.

And so, Milo and Benny lived a long and happy life, always grateful for the friendship they shared and the lessons they learned along the way.

John and Tom

Once upon a time, in a small village, there were two best friends, John and Tom. John was a farmer's son, while Tom was the son of a blacksmith. They were always together, and everyone in the village knew that they were inseparable.

One day, while playing near a river, John slipped and fell into the water. He was struggling to stay afloat when Tom saw him and immediately jumped into the water to save him. Tom pulled John out of the water, but he was shivering and weak. Tom knew that he had to act fast, so he carried John to his house, which was nearby.

Tom's mother, Mrs. Brown, saw them and quickly realized what had happened. She welcomed them and helped John to warm up.

She also gave them some warm milk and cookies to help them feel better. John was grateful for Tom's help and thanked him for saving his life.

From that day on, John and Tom's friendship grew stronger. They did everything together, from playing in the fields to helping each other with their homework. They were always there for each other, no matter what.

Years went by, and John and Tom grew up. They went to different schools, but they still remained close friends. They even helped each other in finding jobs and building their careers.

One day, John got very sick, and he was hospitalized. Tom visited him every day and prayed for his recovery. He even took care of John's farm and animals while he was away. John recovered after a few weeks, and he knew that he had a true friend in Tom.

In the end, John and Tom's friendship was tested many times, but it never faltered. They remained best friends for their entire lives, and everyone in the village looked up to them as an example of true friendship. They showed that true friends are always there for each other, no matter what.

The painter girl

Once upon a time, there was a little girl named Emily. Emily was an orphan who had lost her parents when she was very young. She lived in a small orphanage with other children, but she often felt alone and sad.

Emily had always dreamed of having a family of her own, but she didn't think it was possible. She felt like no one would want to adopt an orphaned girl like her.

One day, a kind and loving couple came to the orphanage looking to adopt a child. Emily was excited but also scared. She didn't want to get her hopes up only to be disappointed.

The couple met with Emily and talked to her about their lives and their hopes for a family. They listened to Emily's story and her dreams. Emily felt like they truly cared about her and her future.

After much consideration, the couple decided to adopt Emily. Emily was overjoyed and couldn't believe that she was finally going to have a family of her own.

As Emily got to know her new family, she realized that they were just what she had always wanted. They loved her unconditionally and supported her in everything she did. They encouraged her to pursue her passions and follow her dreams.

With her new family by her side, Emily began to see a brighter future for herself. She worked hard in school and discovered that she had a talent for art.

She started to create beautiful paintings and drawings that captured the beauty of the world around her.

Emily knew that she had a second chance at happiness and was determined to make the most of it. She wanted to show others that no matter how difficult life may seem, there is always hope for a better tomorrow.

And so, Emily's story became an inspiration to other children who may be struggling. She showed them that no matter how sad or alone they may feel, there is always the possibility of finding love and happiness.

Jungle kid

Once upon a time, in a dense jungle, there lived a young boy named Raj. Raj was born and raised in the jungle and had never seen the outside world. He lived with his family, a group of monkeys who had taken him in when he was a baby.

Growing up, Raj learned to survive in the jungle by observing his monkey family. He learned to climb trees, swing from branch to branch, and find food in the wild. He loved the jungle and all its creatures, and he felt at home among the trees.

One day, a group of travelers stumbled upon Raj's jungle. They were amazed to see a young boy living among the monkeys, and they decided to take him back with them to their village.

At first, Raj was scared and overwhelmed by the new environment. He missed his monkey family and the familiarity of the jungle. But he quickly adapted to his new surroundings and began to explore the village.

Raj was fascinated by all the new things he saw. He saw people walking on two legs, riding horses, and building houses. He was curious about everything and eager to learn more.

Despite the challenges he faced, Raj never gave up. He worked hard to learn the ways of the village, and he quickly became a beloved member of the community. He even taught the villagers some of the things he had learned in the jungle, like how to climb trees and find food in the wild.

Over time, Raj realized that his unique upbringing in the jungle had given him special skills and abilities that he could use to help others. He became a skilled tracker and guide, helping travelers navigate the jungle safely. He also became an ambassador for the animals, teaching others about the importance of protecting the jungle and its creatures.

In the end, Raj's journey from the jungle to the village taught him that even in the most challenging of circumstances, we can find our place in the world and use our unique talents to make a difference. And his inspiring story showed others that no matter where we come from, we all have something valuable to offer.

Magic paintbrush

Once upon a time, in a land far away, there was a young girl named Zara. Zara lived in a world where colors didn't exist. The world was dull and gray, and the people had forgotten what it was like to live in a colorful world.

Zara loved to paint, even though she had never seen colors before. She would imagine what the colors would look like and paint her world with them. Her paintings were beautiful, and they brought joy to everyone who saw them.

One day, Zara discovered a magic paintbrush that could bring color to the world. Excited by the possibilities, she started painting everything around her, and soon the world was filled with vibrant colors.

The people were amazed by the beauty around them, and they began to see the world in a new light. They started to appreciate the little things, like the blue of the sky and the green of the grass.

Zara became known as the girl who brought color to the world. She continued to paint, and her paintings became even more beautiful. She showed the people that anything was possible, even in a world where colors didn't exist.

As time passed, the people started to forget how dull their world had once been.

They took the colors for granted and stopped appreciating them. Zara was saddened by this, but she didn't give up.

She continued to paint, and her paintings became more powerful than ever. She painted stories of hope and courage, and the people were inspired by them. They started to see the world in a new light, and they appreciated the beauty around them once again.

In the end, Zara's paintings brought the world together.

They reminded the people that even in the darkest of times, there is always a glimmer of hope. And her inspiring story taught children that no matter how impossible things may seem, with creativity and imagination, anything is possible.

Technology

Once upon a time, in a world of technology and innovation, there was a young girl named Ava. Ava loved nothing more than coding and programming. She spent all her free time learning about the latest advancements in technology and dreaming up new ideas for her own inventions.

Despite her passion, Ava often felt like an outsider. Her classmates didn't share her interests, and she struggled to find friends who could relate to her love of coding.

One day, Ava stumbled upon a coding competition online. She was hesitant at first, but something inside her told her to give it a try.

She poured all her energy into her entry, determined to showcase her skills to the world.

When the results came in, Ava was shocked to see that she had won first place! She couldn't believe it. For the first time in a long time, she felt like she belonged somewhere.

The win opened up new doors for Ava. She was invited to speak at conferences, meet other young coders, and even collaborate with established tech companies. Her innovative ideas and fresh perspective caught the attention of many in the industry, and she quickly became a rising star.

As her success grew, Ava realized that she could use her platform to help others. She started teaching coding to children in her community, hoping to inspire a new generation of tech-savvy kids. Her classes quickly became popular, and she watched as her students discovered their own love for coding and programming.

Ava's story showed children that no matter how different they may feel, they have unique talents and passions that can lead to amazing things. With hard work and determination, they can accomplish anything they set their minds to, and even use their success to make a positive impact on the world around them.

Adventurous boy

Once upon a time, in a small village in the mountains, there lived a young boy named Kai. Kai was a curious and adventurous boy who loved exploring the world around him.

One day, Kai heard about a mysterious mountain peak that nobody had ever climbed before. The villagers believed that the peak was cursed and that whoever attempted to climb it would never return.

Despite the warnings, Kai was determined to climb the peak and prove everyone wrong. He spent months preparing for the climb, training his body and mind to be strong enough to face the challenges ahead.

On the day of the climb, Kai set out early in the morning with his climbing gear and supplies. The climb was tough, with treacherous cliffs, deep ravines, and unexpected obstacles at every turn.

But Kai was determined and persevered, using his wits and his strength to overcome each obstacle. As he climbed higher and higher, the view became more breathtaking, and he felt a sense of achievement and satisfaction like never before.

Finally, after a long and challenging journey, Kai reached the summit. He felt a sense of pride and accomplishment, knowing that he had achieved what many thought was impossible.

As he looked out at the stunning view from the top, Kai realized that sometimes the greatest rewards come from taking risks and facing your fears. He returned to the village a hero, inspiring other boys to dream big and to never give up on their goals.

Kai's determination and bravery serve as an inspiration to all boys who face challenges in their lives, showing them that with hard work and a never-give-up attitude, they can achieve anything they set their minds to.

Prince William

Once upon a time, in a far-off kingdom, there lived a brave and heroic prince named William. Prince William was known throughout the land for his kindness, wisdom, and his unwavering courage.

One day, a wicked dragon attacked the kingdom, causing destruction and chaos wherever it went. The people of the kingdom were terrified, and they knew that they needed someone brave and courageous to face the dragon and save them.

Without hesitation, Prince William stepped forward, determined to save his kingdom and his people. He rode out to the dragon's lair, armed with only his sword and his courage.

The dragon was huge, with fiery eyes and razor-sharp teeth. It breathed flames and smoke, causing the ground to shake with every roar.

But Prince William was not afraid. He faced the dragon head-on, his sword glinting in the sunlight. He fought fiercely, dodging the dragon's flames and striking it with his sword.

The battle was long and difficult, but Prince William refused to give up. He fought with all his might, determined to save his kingdom and defeat the dragon.

Finally, with one mighty blow, Prince William struck the dragon's heart, and it fell to the ground, defeated.

The people of the kingdom cheered and celebrated their hero. They knew that without Prince William's bravery and courage, their kingdom would have been destroyed.

From that day on, Prince William was known throughout the land as a hero, and his legend lived on for generations. He inspired children to be brave and courageous, to always stand up for what is right, and to never give up in the face of adversity.

Rabbit and fox

Once upon a time, in a field surrounded by tall grass and wildflowers, there lived a brave little rabbit named Benny. Benny was small, but he was quick and agile, and he loved to explore the world around him.

One day, while out foraging for food, Benny heard a faint cry for help. Curious, he followed the sound until he found a small bird trapped in a snare, unable to free herself.

Without hesitation, Benny knew he had to act fast. He carefully approached the bird, using his sharp teeth to cut through the snare, freeing her from her trap. The bird was grateful to Benny, and they quickly became friends.

As they explored the field together, they came across a group of animals who were being bullied by a mean and vicious fox. The animals were afraid and didn't know what to do.

But Benny was not one to back down from a challenge. He decided to help the animals and confront the fox.

With his friend the bird by his side, Benny bravely approached the fox. The fox snarled and bared his teeth, ready to attack. But Benny stood his ground, determined to protect the animals.

The battle was long and fierce, but Benny never gave up. He dodged and weaved, using his speed and agility to outsmart the fox. Finally, with one swift kick, he sent the fox running away, defeated and humiliated.

From that day on, Benny was known as a hero throughout the field. His bravery and his courage inspired animals everywhere, and his name became synonymous with strength and kindness.

And although he faced many challenges in his life, Benny knew that as long as he stayed true to himself and his beliefs, he could overcome anything that came his way.

Tiger Tito

Once upon a time, in a dense jungle surrounded by towering trees and lush greenery, lived a little tiger named Tito. Tito was no ordinary tiger - he was small and weak compared to the other tigers in the jungle, and he was often teased and bullied by them.

But Tito refused to let their taunts and jeers get to him. He knew that he was capable of great things, even though he was small.

One day, as he was wandering through the jungle, Tito came across a group of animals who were in trouble. They were trapped in a net, unable to free themselves.

Despite his small size, Tito knew he had to help. He bravely approached the net and started to gnaw at the ropes, using his sharp teeth to cut through them.

It was slow going, and Tito's jaw ached from the effort, but he refused to give up. Finally, after what seemed like hours, he managed to cut through the last rope, freeing the animals from the net.

The animals were overjoyed and grateful to Tito for his bravery. They thanked him and promised to remember his kind deed.

From that day on, Tito's reputation in the jungle changed. The other animals looked up to him and admired his bravery, and he was no longer teased and bullied by the other tigers.

Tito learned that it didn't matter how big or small he was, what mattered was his heart and his willingness to help others. And although he faced many challenges in his life, he knew that as long as he stayed true to himself and his beliefs, he could overcome anything that came his way.

The end

As we come to the end of this book of inspiring stories for children, we hope that you have been encouraged and inspired by the journeys of these remarkable individuals. Each of these stories is a testament to the power of perseverance, determination, and the belief in oneself.

Through the pages of this book, we have learned about individuals who have overcome incredible odds and achieved great success in their respective fields. Their stories are a reminder that anything is possible if we are willing to work hard and never give up on our dreams.

We hope that these stories have instilled in you a sense of hope and a belief in your own potential. No matter what challenges you may face in your life, remember that you have the strength and resilience to overcome them and achieve your goals.

As you go forward from here, we encourage you to keep these inspiring stories in your heart and to use them as a source of motivation and inspiration in your own life. Remember that you too have the power to make a difference in the world, and that anything is possible if you believe in yourself.

Thank you for joining us on this journey of discovery and inspiration. We hope that these stories will continue to inspire and empower you for years to come.**NASHWAN HASAN**

Contents